How Plants and Animals Reproduce and Adapt?

Houghton Mifflin Harcourt™

PHOTOGRAPHY CREDITS: COVER ©foryouinf/Shutterstock; 4 (bl) ©Vishnevskiy Vasily/
Shutterstock; 4 (t) ©Petra Barz/Panther Media/Age Fotostock; 5 (br) Dean Uhlinger/
Corbis; 8 (t) Elyse Butler/Aurora/Getty Images; 9 (b) ©Manfred Grebler/Alamy Images; 12
(bg) ©Ralph Lee Hopkins/Lonely Planet Images/Getty Images; 13 (b) ©Crystal Garner/
Cutcaster; 13 (t) ©FloridaStock/Shutterstock; 14 (tr) ©PhotoDisc/Getty Images Royalty Free;
14 (bl) ©Mircea Bezergheanu/Shutterstock; 15 (b) ©Jupiterimages/Getty Images; 16 (r)
©foryouinf/Shutterstock; 17 (t) ©Arto Hakola/Shutterstock; 18 (r) ©Janice Lichtenberger/
StockPile Collection/Alamy Images; 19 (b) ©Jupiterimages/Getty Images; 20 (r) ©Igor
Kovalenko/Shutterstock; 21 (t) ©Jeff Rotman/Peter Arnold/Getty Images

ISBN: 978-0-544-07311-1

13 14 15 16 17 18 19 20   1083   20 19 18

4500710587   A B C D E F G

Be an Active Reader!

Look for each word in yellow along with its meaning.

fertilization   incomplete   physical adaptation

pollination   metamorphosis   behavioral adaptation

germination   environment   instinct

complete   adaptation   heredity

   metamorphosis

Underlined sentences answer the questions.

How do plants reproduce?

How do pollen, seeds, and spores travel?

What is the life cycle of a seed plant?

How do animals reproduce?

What is metamorphosis?

Why must a living thing adapt to its environment?

What are physical adaptations?

What are behavioral adaptations?

What is heredity?

What's the difference between instinct and learned behavior?

How do plants reproduce?

Plants grow all over Earth. Cactus plants grow in deserts. Palm trees and orchids grow in rain forests. Mosses grow in swamps. You can find plants growing in cities. Do you wonder how plants reproduce?

Most seed plants reproduce through sexual reproduction. Sperm are the male sex cells. Eggs are the female sex cells. Look at the flower diagram below. Pollen is found in the anther and contains sperm. Eggs are found in the pistil. Many flowers have anthers and a pistil.

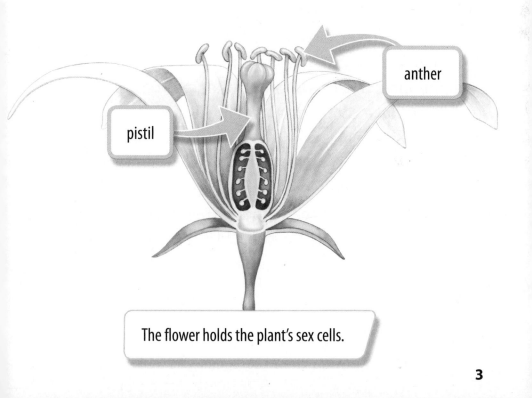

anther

pistil

The flower holds the plant's sex cells.

spore capsule

Moss spores form inside capsules. The capsules grow at the ends of stalks.

Fertilization is the joining of an egg and a sperm. When an egg is fertilized, it grows into an embryo. The embryo forms inside a seed. The embryo is the first stage of a plant's life.

In most seed plants, the seeds form in flowers. For example, apple tree seeds form in the tree's flowers. Other seed plants have cones instead of flowers. For example, seeds of pine trees form in cones.

Some plants don't make seeds. For example, mosses and ferns don't make seeds. Instead, these plants make spores. A spore is a structure that can produce new plants. The spores form inside a capsule. The capsule bursts open and releases the spores.

How do pollen, seeds, and spores travel?

Pollination is the transfer of pollen from the anthers to the pistil of a seed plant. How does the pollen get to the pistil? Both wind and water can carry pollen. Animals can also carry pollen. The bee is one animal that carries pollen. A bee goes from flower to flower to drink nectar. Along the way, the bee picks up pollen from anthers. It leaves behind pollen on the pistil. That's how flowers are pollinated.

Like pollen, seeds travel by wind, water, and animals. Animals transport seeds when they eat fruits. The seeds leave the animals' bodies in their waste. Some seeds have thorns or hooks. These attach to an animal's fur and travel on its body.

Like pollen and seeds, spores travel by wind. Many land in places with good light and water. These spores can then grow into new plants.

Wind carries the pollen of grasses and trees.

What is the life cycle of a seed plant?

Plants grow in stages. A seed plant goes through stages in its life. All the stages together make up a life cycle. A seed is planted in soil. Next, the seed grows into a tiny plant. The plant grows until it can make flowers or cones. These are the parts that make more seeds.

Let's look at the radish life cycle. The radish seed holds the embryo of a radish plant. Germination is the stage when the seed sprouts. When the seed sprouts, the embryo in the seed grows into a tiny plant.

The radish plant gets larger and grows more roots. Then it grows to its full size. It reaches maturity, the stage at which an organism can reproduce. Mature plants make seeds that grow into new plants.

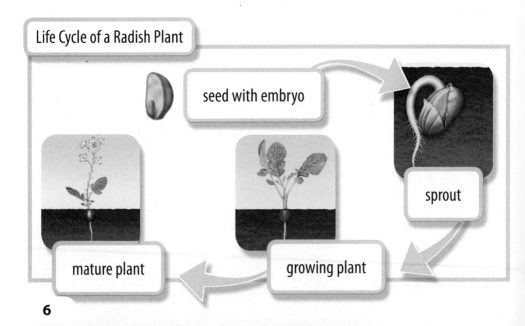

Life Cycle of a Radish Plant

seed with embryo

sprout

mature plant

growing plant

6

We get food from plants. You might grow a plant, such as a lima bean plant, in a garden. Here is how to do it.

First, get a package of lima bean seeds. Next, plant the seeds in soil. Plant them where they'll get a lot of light. The seeds will grow into plants. The plants get bigger and make flowers. Then the bean pods form. The plants are now mature. Each pod holds seeds. We call the seeds beans. The seeds can be planted. They can grow into new lima bean plants.

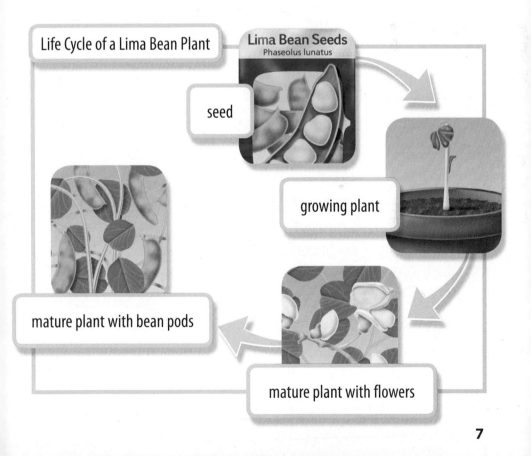

Life Cycle of a Lima Bean Plant

Lima Bean Seeds
Phaseolus lunatus

seed

growing plant

mature plant with bean pods

mature plant with flowers

The temperature of alligator eggs causes the young alligators to be male or female.

How do animals reproduce?

Most animals reproduce sexually. A sperm from a male joins with an egg from a female. The fertilized egg grows into a new animal.

The eggs of some animals are fertilized outside the female's body. This happens with frogs. The eggs of some other animals are fertilized inside the female's body. This happens with alligators. The female alligator builds a nest with leaves and grasses. Then she lays her eggs. She covers the eggs with more leaves and grass. She watches over the nest.

The eggs are in the nest for about two months. Then the young begin to squeak. That's the sign that they are ready to hatch. Once they hatch, the female carries the young to the water. She carries them in her mouth. When alligators are 10 years old, they can mate and produce young.

Other animals don't lay eggs. The female gives birth to live young. She cares for the young and feeds them milk. Lions, cows, and dogs are born this way.

Female horses give birth to live babies. They care for the babies and feed them milk.

What is metamorphosis?

Look back at the young alligator and horse in the pictures. Do they look like the adult animals? With some animals, the young look very different. These animals go through complete metamorphosis.

In complete metamorphosis, animals go through four stages in their life cycle. Examples of these animals are butterflies and beetles. A butterfly egg hatches into a larva. The larva is a caterpillar. The caterpillar looks different from the butterfly. Next, the caterpillar becomes a pupa inside a chrysalis. Then the pupa becomes an adult butterfly. The butterfly splits open the chrysalis and flies out.

egg

Butterflies go through complete metamorphosis.

adult butterfly

larva

pupa

Some insects go through a different life cycle called incomplete metamorphosis. A dragonfly is an example. In incomplete metamorphosis, there are three stages of development.

A dragonfly hatches from its egg. It is a nymph, an immature form. The nymph looks like an adult dragonfly but doesn't have wings. The nymph grows larger. It molts, or sheds its outer covering. It molts several times. Then it grows wings. It is at the adult stage. It looks and acts like an adult dragonfly.

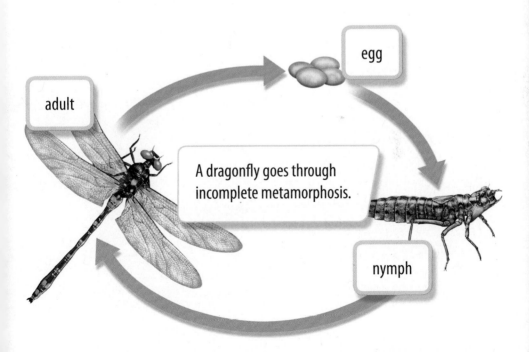

egg

adult

A dragonfly goes through incomplete metamorphosis.

nymph

Why must a living thing adapt to its environment?

Deserts and rain forests are environments. An environment is all the living and nonliving things that surround and affect an organism. Look at the picture below. It shows a wetland environment. The environment includes plants, animals, water, air, and land.

All living things need air, water, and food. Animals need shelter, too. A plant or animal gets the things it needs from its environment.

Birds and other animals live in wetlands. They find air, food, water, and a safe place to live.

Earth has many different environments. Deserts have little rainfall. Rain forests are hot and have a large amount of rainfall. The Arctic is very cold. Each living thing must be able to stay alive in its environment.

An adaptation is a trait or characteristic that helps an organism survive. Adaptations help each organism stay alive in its environment. The saguaro cactus is a plant with a large root system. The root system spreads far from the plant's trunk to help the cactus collect rainfall. The root system helps the cactus stay alive in the desert. It is an adaptation.

Saguaro cactus plants have adaptations that help them live with little water.

water lily

Water lilies have adaptations that help them live in water.

What are physical adaptations?

A physical adaptation is an adaptation in a body part. A macaw is a parrot. It lives in the rain forest. A macaw has a large, powerful beak. Its beak helps the bird break open nuts and seeds. The macaw also has toes that help it grip tree branches. The toes can also hold objects. The macaw's beak and feet are physical adaptations.

A mallard is a type of duck. It has physical adaptations that help it live in water. The mallard has a flat beak called a bill. The bill helps it catch food underwater. The mallard also has webbed feet. These feet help it move quickly on and under water.

macaw

mallard

Beaks and bills are important body parts. They help birds find and eat food.

Polar bears live in the freezing Arctic. They have physical adaptations that help them survive there. Polar bears have long snouts that help them poke into holes in the ice. Then they pull out their favorite meal—a seal. Polar bears also have wide feet with claws. These feet help them walk on ice without slipping.

Camels live in the desert. There, most plants are tough. The plants have sharp points on their stems. Camels have a physical adaptation that helps them eat the plants. They have sharp teeth. Camels also have wide feet. This adaptation helps them walk on sand without sinking.

Look at the picture of the desert. What else might a camel need to stay alive in this environment?

What are behavioral adaptations?

A behavioral adaptation is something an animal does that helps it survive. Have you seen emperor penguins on TV or in a movie? You probably saw how the males gather into a tight group. The males do this to stay warm. This is a behavioral adaptation.

An instinct is a behavioral adaptation. An instinct is a behavior that does not have to be learned. Many Arctic animals dig dens in the snow. They live in the dens during the coldest time of year. Some desert animals dig dens in the sand. They spend the hottest part of the day in their den. The animals do these things by instinct.

Sea turtles hatch on land. The baby turtles move toward light over the open ocean. This is an example of instinct.

Arctic terns fly from the Arctic to Antarctica, and back, every year. This is a behavioral adaptation.

Bears have behavioral adaptations that help them in winter. At the end of the summer, bears start to eat a lot. Each day, they eat five times as much as they usually do. They do this until the end of fall. Eating all that food adds a layer of fat to their body. Then they look for a place to spend the winter. It might be a big hole in a tree. The bears spend the winter in this den. They don't come out to eat or drink. They live on their stored fat.

Humpback whales live off the coast of Alaska. In fall, they leave this home. They swim to warm ocean waters near Hawaii. That's where they spend the winter. They also give birth to their young there. In the spring, they go back to the Alaskan coast.

What is heredity?

Heredity is the passing of traits from parents to their offspring. All living things pass traits on to their young. Plants pass traits on such as flower color. Animals pass traits on, too. That is why animal family members look like each other. For example, a young tiger gets its striped coat from its parents.

Every living thing has genes. Genes are in sex cells. A male sex cell and a female sex cell join and form a new cell. The new cell has genes from both the female cell

Most skunks have black and white fur. This is passed on from their parents.

and the male cell. Genes are the chemical instructions that control traits. In animals that use sexual reproduction, half of a living thing's traits come from the mother. Half come from the father.

An environment can change the traits of living things. Here's one example. Tadpoles are frog larvae. They swim in ponds. A pond will dry up without rain. If this happens, the tadpoles quickly become adult frogs. They become adults faster than tadpoles living in a pond that does not dry out.

Temperature can also change living things. You learned that temperature affects the eggs in an alligator nest. If it's 86 °Fahrenheit (°F) or less, the young will be female. If it's 93 °F or more, the young will be male. Between 86 °F and 93 °F, there will be a mix of male and female alligators.

Light can change living things. These sunflowers grow toward the light.

What's the difference between instinct and learned behavior?

Animals can learn to act in certain ways. They can learn to do different things. Learning helps animals live. A learned behavior is something an animal learns to do. The animal might learn it by watching other animals.

Instincts are behaviors that animals are born with. They are not learned. Instincts help animals live and stay safe. If a rattlesnake is trapped, it will likely rattle its tail. This is a warning to stay away. It is an instinct.

The American White Pelican catches fish with its large bill. This behavior is instinct.

Each fall, monarch butterflies fly south. They go from the United States to Mexico. They want to be where it is warm. In the spring, they fly back. No one teaches them to do this. It is an instinct. Many types of birds also know by instinct to fly to a warmer place for winter.

The mother dolphin whistles to her young. The calf learns to recognize its mother.

When geese hatch, the parent is the first living thing they see. Young geese follow their mother everywhere. This is instinct. They watch their parents. They learn how the parents get food.

Animals can learn more difficult things. Young coyotes learn to hunt from older coyotes. They also learn how to be part of a pack. Young prairie dogs watch adult family members. They learn how to protect themselves. They learn to recognize a danger call. When they hear it, they find a safe place to hide.

Model an Environmental Change

With a partner, gather these materials: shoebox with lid, cardboard, scissors, tape, and a small potted plant. Cut a large hole in one end of the shoebox. Then cut two pieces of cardboard. They should be the same height and half the width of the box. Tape one piece to the inside of the shoebox. It should be about one-third of the way down the box. Tape the other piece inside the shoebox on the opposite side. It should be about two-thirds of the way down the box. Stand the box so that the hole is at the top. Place the plant in the box. Be sure it is watered. Tape the lid of the box on tightly. Wait 5 days and then open the box. You'll see how light affects a plant's growth.

Write an Article

Write an article for a website. First, choose an animal. Use the Internet and books to learn about the animal. Find out what adaptations the animal has to help it live in its environment.

Glossary

adaptation [ad•uhp•TAY•shuhn] A trait or characteristic that helps an organism survive. *A polar bear's feet are an adaptation to its environment.*

behavioral adaptation [bih•HAYV•yu•ruhl ad•uhp•TAY•shuhn] Something an animal does that helps it survive. *Finding warm weather in winter is a behavioral adaptation.*

complete metamorphosis [kuhm•PLEET met•uh•MAWR•fuh•sis] A complex change that most insects undergo that includes larva and pupa stages. *In complete metamorphosis, animals grow in four stages.*

environment [en•VY•ruhn•muhnt] All the living and nonliving things that surround and affect an organism. *Some animals eat the plants in a rain forest environment.*

fertilization [fer•tl•li•ZAY•shuhn] The joining together of a sperm and an egg cell. *There must be a male and a female sex cell for fertilization to take place.*

germination [jer•muh•NAY•shuhn] The sprouting of a seed. *When germination happens, a young plant appears.*

heredity [huh•RED•ih•tee] The process by which traits are passed from parents to offspring. *Because of heredity, animals look like their parents.*

incomplete metamorphosis [in•kuhm•PLEET met•uh•MAWR•fuh•sis] Developmental change in some insects in which a nymph hatches from an egg and gradually develops into an adult. *In incomplete metamorphosis, insects grow in three stages.*

instinct [IN•stinkt] A behavior an animal knows how to do without having to learn it. *Horses have the instinct to stand and walk after they are born.*

physical adaptation [FIZ•ih•kuhl ad•uhp•TAY•shuhn] An adaptation to a body part. *A sharp, strong beak is a physical adaptation.*

pollination [pol•uh•NAY•shuhn] The transfer of pollen from a male plant part to a female plant part of seed plants. *Pollination happens when bees go from flower to flower.*